THE
GREAT GREEN
FOREST

Paul Geraghty

RED FOX

High up in the great green forest, the sun began to rise.

Way down in the deep dark shadows, a treemouse
was curling up to sleep.

Creech! Creech! Woop! Woop! chirped the frogs. The sounds were screechy, the sounds were sharp: *Woopoo! Woopoo! Creech! Creech!*

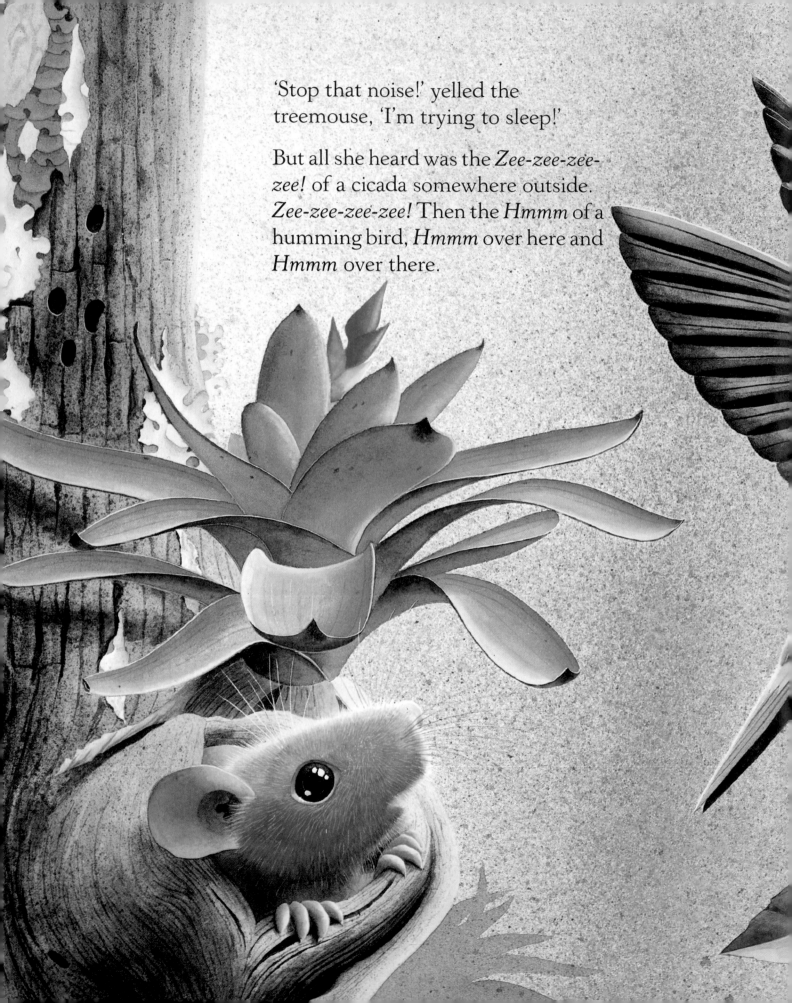

'Stop that noise!' yelled the treemouse, 'I'm trying to sleep!'

But all she heard was the *Zee-zee-zee-zee!* of a cicada somewhere outside. *Zee-zee-zee-zee!* Then the *Hmmm* of a humming bird, *Hmmm* over here and *Hmmm* over there.

'Stop that noise!' yelled the treemouse, 'I'm trying to sleep!'

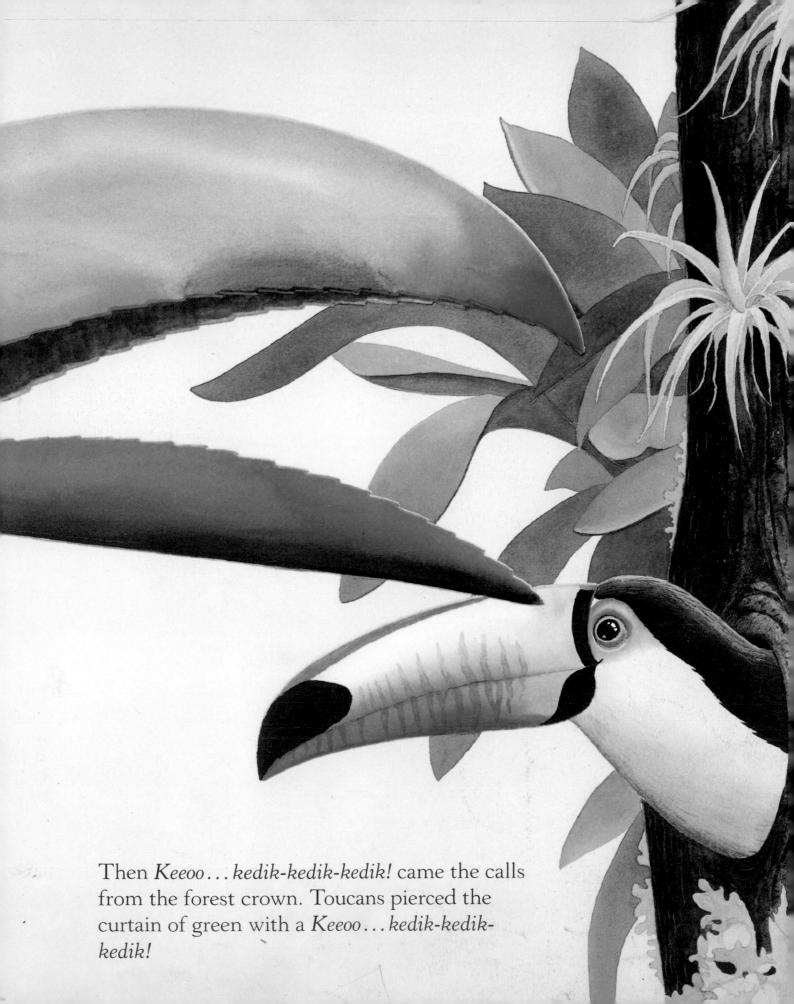

Then *Keeoo...kedik-kedik-kedik!* came the calls
from the forest crown. Toucans pierced the
curtain of green with a *Keeoo...kedik-kedik-
kedik!*

'Stop that noise!' yelled the treemouse, 'I'm trying to sleep!' But the forest was alive with songs and sounds.

Yaag! Screecha-screecha-screecha! squawked a macaw, *Yaag! SCRAAA! SCRAAA!* squawked another.

'Stop that noise!' yelled the treemouse, 'I'm trying to sleep!'

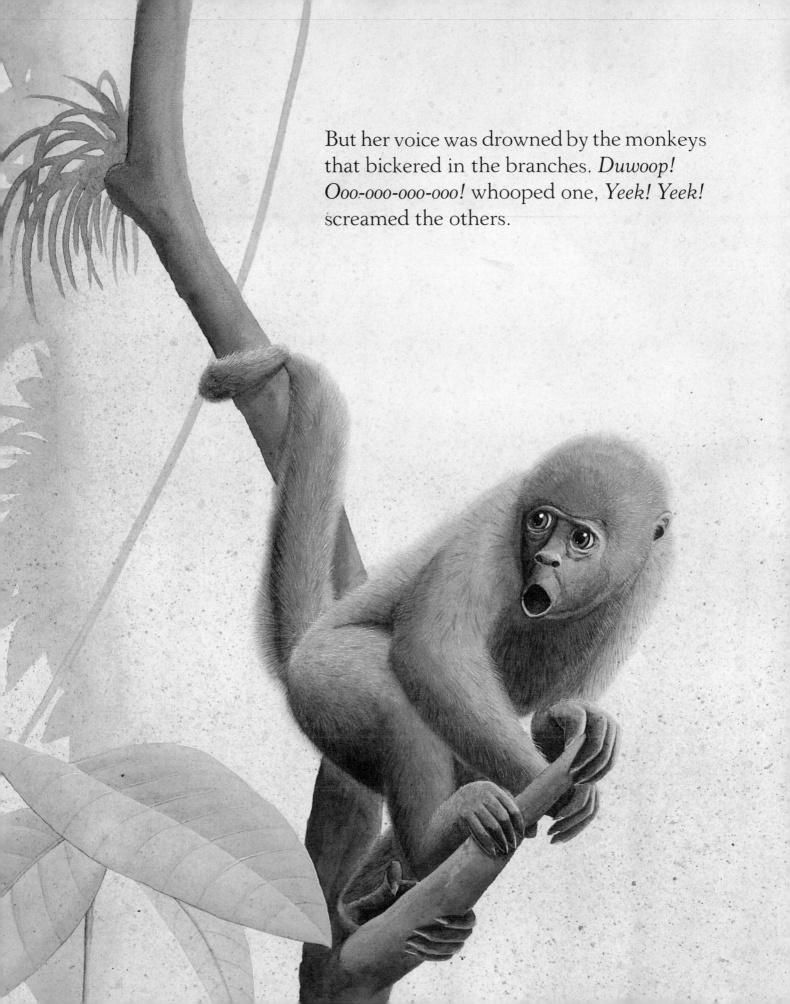

But her voice was drowned by the monkeys that bickered in the branches. *Duwoop! Ooo-ooo-ooo-ooo!* whooped one, *Yeek! Yeek!* screamed the others.

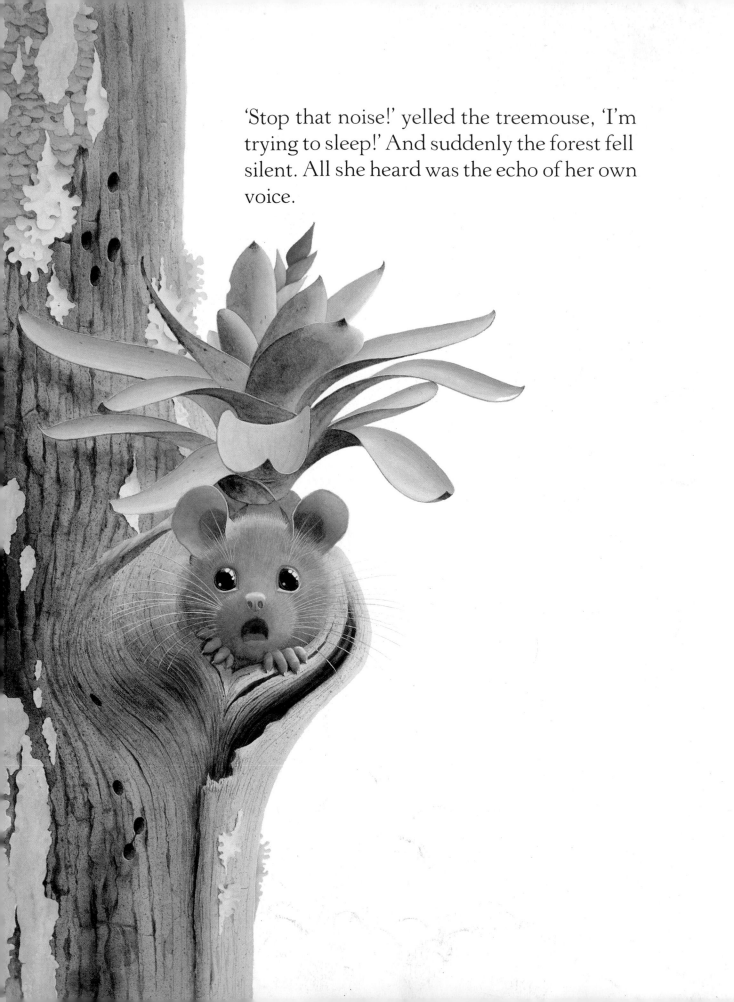

'Stop that noise!' yelled the treemouse, 'I'm trying to sleep!' And suddenly the forest fell silent. All she heard was the echo of her own voice.

Animals clung in silence, not daring to move or make a sound.

Even the cats that ruled the forest now cowered in the quiet. That's better! thought the treemouse.

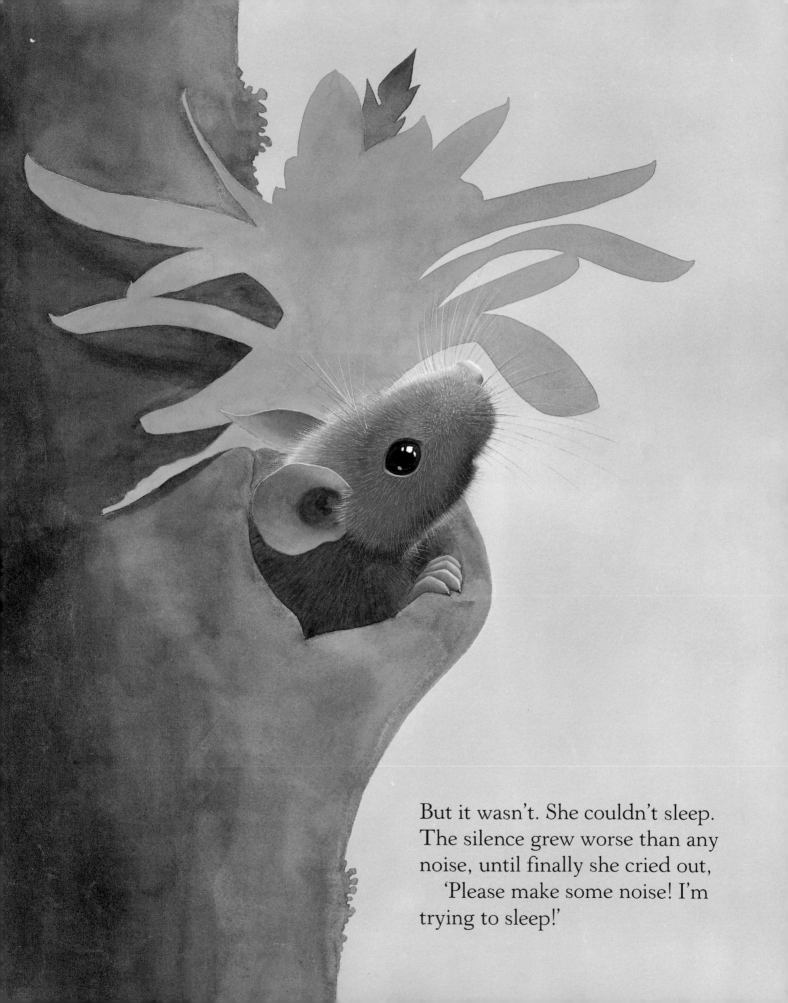

But it wasn't. She couldn't sleep.
The silence grew worse than any
noise, until finally she cried out,
    'Please make some noise! I'm
trying to sleep!'

She waited. And then there was a noise. She heard a distant *Brrrm, brrrm . . .* and then a *C-r-r-r-r-r-RACKA-DACKA-RACKA* **SHOONG**! that shook her to the ground.

A tree had fallen. And a gaping hole was left in the crown of the great green forest.

C-r-r-r-r-r-RACKA-DACKA-RACKA
SHOONG!
Another tree came down!

Brrrm, BRRRM . . . an ugly sound made the ground shudder. And the treemouse knew her tree would be next.

She looked up at her home; then she turned to the terrible sound. And at the top of her voice she yelled, 'STOP THAT NOISE!'

But that noise didn't stop.
Brrrm, it drew closer, *BRRRM,* till the earth
thundered; *BRRRM!* it grew louder, **BRRRM!**
till the earth shook. But the treemouse stood
firm.

Then something made the driver stop. And when he stopped, he felt the silence. He saw the broken trees. He saw the fallen nests.

And he sensed angry eyes watching him.

So he sat and he thought. He stayed there and thought till
the sun went down. And when it was dark, he went away.

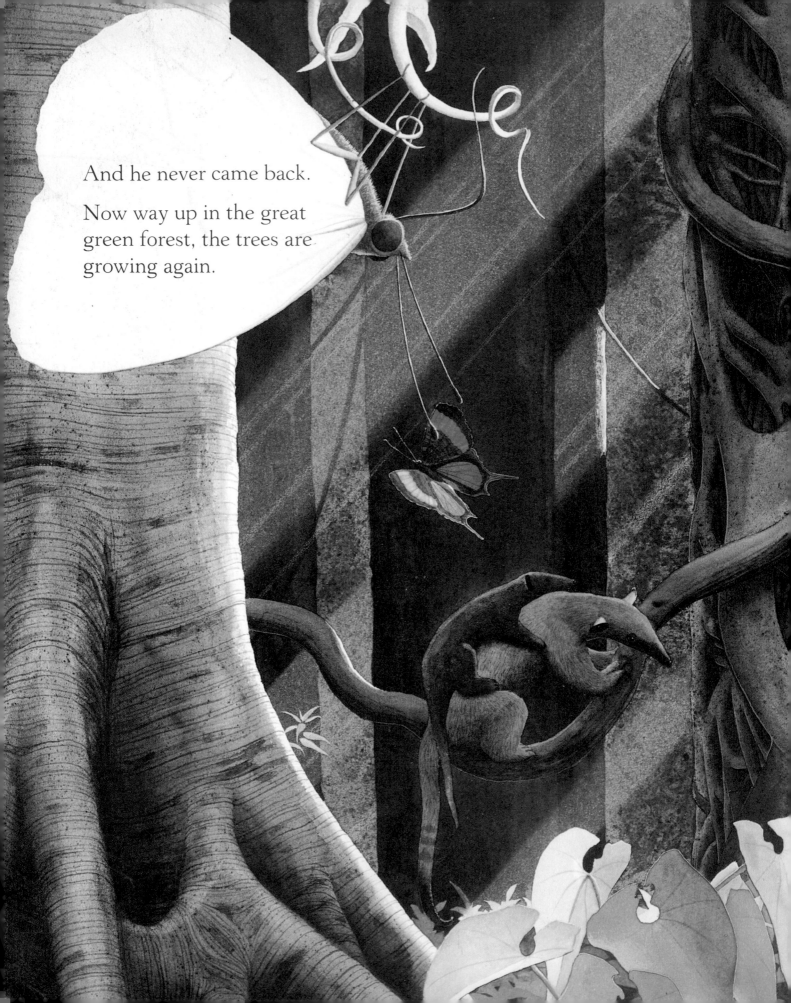

And he never came back.

Now way up in the great green forest, the trees are growing again.

And deep down in the dark shadows, a treemouse curls up and closes her eyes. She listens to the songs and sounds of the forest, which tell her that, for now, she can sleep in peace.